Horses Her Way

A BRISA STORY

By Sibley Miller

Illustrated by Tara Larsen Chang and Jo Gershman

Feiwel and Friends

For Shoshana and Marco—Sibley Miller

To "baby" Michael—for Web camera inspiration. Ah ha
HA!—Tara Larsen Chang

To Muriel and Myron for your wholehearted support
since the day we met—Jo Gershman

A FEIWEL AND FRIENDS BOOK
An Imprint of Macmillan

WIND DANCERS: HORSES HER WAY. Copyright © 2009
by Reeves International, Inc. All rights reserved. BREYER,
WIND DANCERS, and BREYER logos are trademarks and/or registered
trademarks of Reeves International, Inc. Printed in August 2009 in China
by Leo Paper, Heshan City, Guangdong Province. For information,
address Feiwel and Friends,
175 Fifth Avenue, New York, N.Y. 10010.

Library of Congress Cataloging-in-Publication Data Available

ISBN: 978-0-312-56279-3

DESIGNED BY BARBARA GRZESLO
Feiwel and Friends logo designed by Filomena Tuosto

First Edition: 2009

1 3 5 7 9 10 8 6 4 2

www.feiwelandfriends.com

CONTENTS

Meet the Wind Dancers

One day, a lonely little girl named Leanna blows on a doozy of a dandelion. To her delight and surprise, four tiny horses spring from the puff of the dandelion seeds!

Four tiny horses with shiny manes and shimmery wings. Four magical horses who can fly!

Dancing on the wind, surrounded by magic halos, they are the Wind Dancers.

The leader of the quartet is Kona. She has a violet-black coat and vivid purple mane, and she flies inside a halo of magical flowers.

Brisa is as pretty as a tropical sunset with her coral-pink color and blonde mane and tail. Magical jewels make up Brisa's halo, and she likes to admire her gems (and herself) every time she looks in a mirror.

Sumatra is silvery blue with sea-green wings. Much like the ocean, she can shift from calm to stormy in a hurry. Her magical halo is made up of ribbons, which flutter and dance as she flies.

The fourth Wind Dancer is—surprise!—a colt. His name is Sirocco. He's a fiery gold, and he likes to go-go-go. Everywhere he goes, his magical halo of butterflies goes, too.

The tiny, flying horses live together in the dandelion meadow in a lovely house carved out of the trunk of an apple tree. Every day, Leanna wishes she'll see the magical little horses again. (She's sure they're nearby, but she doesn't know they're invisible to people.) And the Wind Dancers get ready for their next adventure.

CHAPTER 1

Swim Team

*S*plash!

Two of the three fillies, Kona and Sumatra, were standing ankle-deep in the gentle water of a creek near their apple tree house.

Sirocco, on the other hand, was splashing around smack dab in the *middle* of the creek.

"SIR-OC-CO!" Kona and Sumatra neighed indignantly at their fellow Wind Dancer.

"What?" Sirocco said innocently as he joyfully thrashed in the water.

"This was *supposed* to be just a morning romp," Sumatra reprimanded the unruly colt.

"Right," Kona agreed. "To get our last taste of the creek before it gets too cold."

She glanced up at the tree branches that were hanging over the creek. The leaves were already turning golden yellow and russet red as autumn approached.

"So what's the problem?" Sirocco asked again.

Splash, splash, splash!

Now came a sweet sing-songy voice from the bank of the creek: "You're not romping, Sirocco! You're positively *wallowing* in the water!"

This was Brisa, curled up on a perfect little mound of emerald moss. Her long, blonde mane shimmered. Her coral-pink coat gleamed. And the jewels in her magic halo danced around her.

Sirocco rolled his eyes at the pretty little filly.

"I don't know why it matters to you, Brisa," he said. "You haven't come anywhere *near* the water."

"Of course not!" Brisa said, widening her already huge eyes. "A damp mane? A matted tail? Hooves covered with creek silt? I don't *think* so."

Kona looked down a little sheepishly at the white socks on her forelegs. They were, indeed, mottled with mud.

Sumatra's pale green tail *did* look wet and stringy compared to Brisa's flowing blonde one.

And Sirocco was a complete mess!

But Sirocco didn't care if he was dirty!

And he didn't think his friends should care, either.

"C'mon," he scoffed, using his nose to send a splash Kona's way. "It's our last dip of the season. Live a little!"

The splash hit Kona right between the eyes. She gasped in shock.

And then—she grinned.

"Don't dish it out," she taunted, pulling her foreleg back, "if you can't *take* it."

She kicked the water with all her might. A tiny tidal wave careened toward Sirocco and soaked his mane through.

"Ha!" he shouted. He began kicking water with all *four* of his legs.

"*Ahh!*" Sumatra shrieked, laughing as Sirocco soaked her next. "I'll get you!"

She swatted at the creek with her tail, sending water droplets everywhere.

"*Eek!*" Brisa cried. She fluttered her wings hard and rose into the air. "You guys are going to get me all *dirty*!"

She hovered hesitantly above the creek.

"Aw, come on in, Brisa!" Sirocco called out. He batted his wings against the water, sending a great, silty spray up toward her.

"*Eek!*" Brisa cried again, darting higher into the air. "I brushed my mane with *two* hundred strokes so I'd be twice as beautiful today. You're going to mess it all up!"

Sirocco looked around. There was nobody at the creek besides the Wind Dancers, a few dragonflies, and some minnows.

"Nobody here cares what you look like!" Sirocco bellowed.

"*I* care," Brisa said simply. And with that, she turned and began flying away.

"Don't be angry with us, Brisa," Kona implored.

"Oh, I'm not angry," Brisa assured her friends, fully meaning it. "Anger causes scrunched-up lines around the eyes."

That only made Sirocco roll *his* eyes.

"I'm just going to take a nice, *clean* cruise around the meadow," Brisa called as she flew. "I'll be back when you all are done making messes."

"You're seriously going to miss our last swim of the season?" Sumatra yelled after her.

"Better pretty than gritty!" Brisa called with a laugh. Then, after one last glance at her frolicking friends, she was gone.

. . .

"Tra, la, la, laaaaaa!"

Brisa sang sweetly to herself as she bobbed aimlessly above the dandelion meadow. She was so busy enjoying the breeze and the sun glinting on her halo of jewels that she barely paid attention to where she was flying.

Until suddenly, she spotted a familiar red-brick building right in front of her!

"It's Leanna's school!" Brisa chirped to herself excitedly. "If anybody always looks as pretty as I do, it's Leanna! I'll just peek into her classroom and see what she's up to."

Brisa fluttered over to the open classroom window and peered inside.

"That's our girl," Brisa whispered to herself upon seeing Leanna. "And she's as pretty as always!"

But Brisa was a little wistful. She so wished Leanna could see—and admire—*her* beauty as well.

Before Brisa could get all sad about her invisibility to people, though, Leanna's teacher clapped her hands and made an announcement.

"Class," she said. "For our art lesson today, please draw something that you find beautiful."

"Ooh!" Brisa squeaked. "It's the *perfect* assignment!"

"Draw something lovely from the natural world," the teacher continued. "A tree, clouds in the sky, an animal, whatever you like."

"That's easy!" Leanna and Brisa said at the same time. Brisa giggled at the jinx, as Leanna hurried to the art supply station. She returned a moment later with a tray of pretty pastels and some thick, white paper. Then she began to draw an animal with four elegant legs, a proud arched neck, upstanding ears, a mane, a tail. . . .

"It's a horse!" Brisa cried triumphantly.

She watched Leanna's busy hands, waiting for her to add sparkly wings, a pretty coat, and a magic halo to her picture.

"I wonder if she's drawing *me*," Brisa whispered to herself, hoping to see Leanna color her horse coral pink and surround it with magic jewels.

To Brisa's surprise, Leanna colored her horse a chestnut brown, with a braided mane and tail and a pattern on her rump. But not a single jewel!

I guess Leanna chose to draw one of the big horses, Brisa thought to herself sadly, referring to the Wind Dancers' no-nonsense, non-magical friends who lived in a paddock at the edge of the dandelion meadow. *Not that the big horses aren't pretty, too. But I wonder why—*

"I wish—" Leanna whispered to herself, interrupting Brisa's thoughts. Brisa's silky ears perked up. She found herself flying inside the classroom to get closer.

"I wish," Leanna repeated under her breath, "that I could draw a Wind Dancer along with my horse. But my teacher would never believe that a tiny, flying horse exists in nature. She'd think I made it up!"

Brisa grinned. So Leanna *hadn't* forgotten about her and the other Wind Dancers!

Leanna carefully colored her horse's eye brown. Then she said, "Done!"

"Oh," Brisa whispered in disappointment, as she fluttered back through the window and into the sunshiny day.

"I understand why Leanna couldn't draw a Wind Dancer. And her horse *is* pretty. But why not make it even prettier! Why on *earth* not?"

As Brisa flew back toward home, she gazed around her. Suddenly, she felt like she was looking at the world with new eyes!

And the little idea she'd had for Leanna was turning into a full-fledged brainstorm! And from a brainstorm, it quickly grew into an actual plan! It was the best she'd ever had!

And I want to get started on it right away! Brisa thought to herself in excitement.

Whinnying happily, the filly twisted in the air and flew as fast as she could back to the dandelion meadow.

CHAPTER 2

Make Like a Tree and Leave

"I think I still have some mud caked in my hooves," Sumatra said, peering down at one of her not-so-clean legs. She, Kona, and Sirocco had just finished their dip in the muddy creek.

"And I can*not* seem to get all these snarls out," Kona admitted, frowning at her knotty mane and tail.

The fillies looked expectantly at Sirocco.

But Sirocco just hummed contentedly and did a couple of happy loop-de-loops—until he saw Kona and Sumatra staring at him.

"What?!" he demanded.

"Don't you feel a little scruffy, too?" Kona asked him.

"Naw," Sirocco scoffed. "I feel good!"

The dirt-flecked butterflies in his magic halo nodded in agreement.

"If you ask me, a horse shouldn't fuss too much," Sirocco went on. "It's more important to have fun! Preferably, fun that involves *mud*."

"Don't let Brisa hear you say that," Sumatra said dryly. "She might throw one of her magic jewels at you."

"And make her magic halo one jewel less pretty?" Sirocco scoffed. "I don't *think* so— ow!"

Sirocco stopped short in the air as something hard *thunked* him on his flank.

"What was that?" Sirocco yelled, looking up at a red maple tree.

Something caught Kona's eye and she flew to investigate.

A pretty, cranberry-colored leaf lay on the grass. When Kona flipped it over with her nose, she gasped.

Firmly attached to the leaf was a sparkly silver gem.

A gem that Kona recognized!

"Brisa *did* throw a jewel at you, Sirocco!" Kona said. She peered up at the tree.

"Brisa?" she called.

The branches rustled and suddenly, out popped Brisa's pink-spotted nose.

"Oh, hi there!" Brisa cried in surprise, poking out from a tree branch. "You'll never *guess* what I'm doing!"

"Let's see," Kona said. "Are you . . . using a bucket full of pinesap to glue your magic

jewels to this poor tree's leaves?"

Brisa frowned.

"No, of course not," she said. "Pinesap is way too sticky. It might get in my hair. I'm using *birch* sap."

Sumatra's mouth dropped open and she stared, aghast, at Brisa.

"*What?*" Brisa said innocently—as another ruby leaf suddenly plummeted from the tree and *thwapped* to the ground.

"Brisa!" Sumatra, Kona, and Sirocco all

sputtered together.

Thwap! Another leaf hit the dirt.

"What?" Brisa said again.

"Why in the world would you glue jewels onto perfectly fine leaves?" Sumatra wondered.

"That's just it," Brisa said. She gazed up at the tree dreamily. "These leaves are *only* fine. But they could be *fabulous*. So, I'm helping them along with my jewels."

"You're *dressing up a tree*?" Sirocco asked in astonishment.

"Isn't it beautiful?" Brisa sighed, as she attached jewels to a few more leaves. Then she flew backward to survey her work. The tree *did* glint and glitter in the autumn sunlight.

It also lost three more gem-encrusted leaves.

Thwap! Thwap! Thwap!

Brisa didn't notice.

"See," she pointed out to her friends, "now the tree glints and sparkles in the sunlight. I've made it almost as pretty as me!"

"I'm sure the tree is *truly* grateful," Sirocco said sarcastically.

"I hope so!" Brisa said earnestly. "Making it pretty was hard work. I just hope I don't *look* as tired as I *feel*."

She fluffed up her tail as—*thwap, thwap, thwap*—three more leaves went down.

"Brisa, are you NOTICING ANY-THING?" yelled Sumatra.

"What?" Brisa asked in alarm. She peered over her shoulder to

inspect her coral coat. "Do I have birch sap on my coat? Leaves in my mane? What?!"

Indignantly, Sumatra pointed at the fallen leaves with a front hoof.

"Oh!" Brisa exclaimed as she eyed the sizeable scattering of bejeweled leaves lying on the grass beneath the tree. "Oh, look! A *pile* of jewel-ly leaves! Oh, wouldn't you just *love* to jump in them? Except we'd get all messy, of course."

"Say no more!" Sirocco yelled. He dive-bombed into the leaf pile and emerged with red leaves—not to mention twigs, acorns, and a couple of bugs—twisted into his mane. He and his halo of magic butterflies laughed.

"Sirocco! You're even *more* dirty now!" Brisa cried. "Don't you care?"

"Brisa!" the colt called back teasingly. "Don't *you* care about having fun? Don't you care?"

Brisa faltered for a moment. She gazed down at Sirocco. He *did* look really happy.

But he also looks pretty scraggly, Brisa reminded herself, *and I just* couldn't *let myself go like that—*

"Um, excuse me, pretty filly," Sumatra said, interrupting Brisa's thoughts. "I wasn't pointing out the leaves because they're fun to jump in! There's something wrong here!"

"What's that?" Brisa asked, looking at Sumatra in confusion.

Thwap, *thwap*, *thwap*, went three more leaves falling to the ground.

"Those leaves are on the ground," Sumatra said, pointing at the steadily growing pile on the grass, "but they're *supposed* to be on the tree."

"But isn't that what fall means?" Brisa said, blinking her long, dark lashes. "Leaves *fall* to the ground?"

"Yes, but that's *after* they're ready to fall on their own," Kona said patiently. "The leaves have just changed color. It's not time for them to drop yet."

"Oh!" Brisa squeaked. She hung her head.

"And here I thought I was doing a *good* thing. I wanted to decorate all the other trees in the meadow by nightfall."

"Well," Kona said gently, giving Brisa a comforting nose nuzzle, "maybe you've learned a lesson from this."

Brisa nodded seriously.

"Oh, I sure have," she said. "I've learned that . . . I'm going to have to find something *else* to beautify!"

Suddenly, her pretty brown eyes sparkled with an idea.

"And I know *just* the thing!" she breathed.

"Brisa," Kona protested, "that isn't exactly what I meant—"

But before she could finish her sentence, Brisa had become a pink blur, flying eagerly toward the forest at the edge of the dandelion meadow!

CHAPTER 3
Let Sleeping Frogs Lie

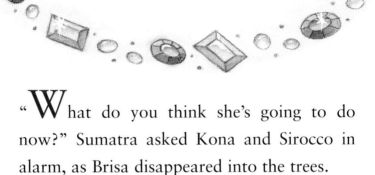

"What do you think she's going to do now?" Sumatra asked Kona and Sirocco in alarm, as Brisa disappeared into the trees.

"Well, whatever she does," Kona said hesitantly, "we know Brisa means well."

"*Meaning* well isn't going to save some poor, unsuspecting trees," Sumatra said.

"Or flowers or birds or bugs or . . ." Sirocco's voice trailed off as he imagined all the forest inhabitants that Brisa might try to make beautiful.

The three Wind Dancers looked at each

other with wide eyes.

"Let's go!" Sirocco said.

The trio zipped into the woods, hot on Brisa's trail, but they weren't quick enough. Their pretty friend was nowhere to be seen.

"Listen for *tra-la-la-la-ing*," Sumatra suggested as they flew deep into the forest.

"Or the *tinkle-tinkle-tinkle* of magic jewels," Kona said.

"Or the utter silence of a filly staying perfectly clean," Sirocco added with an eye-roll.

But then he stopped short in mid-air.

"Hey, what's that?" he said, his voice full of wonder.

Sirocco was staring at the bank of a little creek that ran through the woods. It had white, sandy mud. It wasn't mushy and gushy like brown mud, either. It was thick and solid, yet it still looked moist and inviting.

It was impossible to resist.

Sirocco flew down to the creek and promptly scooped up a clod of the stuff with the front of his hoof. He sniffed at it.

"It's clay!" he announced joyfully. It made a squishing noise and left a big, white splotch between his nostrils. "It's awesome!" Sirocco added. "I could play with this stuff for hours!"

Kona landed next to him.

"We could also use this clay to make things," she said practically. "Dishes and bowls and flowerpots!"

"Or we could use it to . . ." Sirocco scooped up a hoof-full and flung it right at Kona!

Splat!

". . . have a little pre-winter snowball fight!" Sirocco cried.

"Ugh!" Kona neighed in outrage.

"Sirocco!" Sumatra scolded the colt, as she landed on the ground next to her friends. "You shouldn't waste this clay by just throwing it around."

"Oh, yeah?" Sirocco said. A mischievous glint came into his eyes.

"Yeah, oh yeah!" Sumatra declared. Then a mischievous glint came into *her* eyes.

"Not when you could use it," she added, "to do a little *painting*!"

Sumatra dug her nose into the clay and came up with a chunk of it. Then she trotted over to Sirocco and used the clay to blot big, white polka dots all over his side!

Sirocco laughed so hard he fell—right onto the sticky creek bank! The fall covered his *other* side with a single, giant polka dot.

Then he scooped up his own nose-full of clay and smeared a stripe of it down Sumatra's neck.

"Hey, you guys," Kona reprimanded them. "Shouldn't we be thinking about Bri—"

"Get her!" Sumatra neighed to Sirocco.

They covered their noses with more white clay and charged at Kona. Before she knew it, Kona had a messy, white smiley face on her right flank and big, white circles around both her eyes.

This sent all three horses into more fits of laughter. Until—

"Hel-looooo? Anybody home?"

Sirocco jumped, then exclaimed, "That's Brisa!"

Without another word (but not before scooping up an extra clod of clay to take with him), the colt dashed off in the direction of Brisa's voice.

Kona and Sumatra glanced at each other, shrugged, and took off after him.

· · ·

While her friends clobbered each other with white clay, Brisa honed in on her mission—in a gushy, brown mud puddle deep in the forest.

Just as she'd hoped, three sets of bulgy eyes were poking out of the top of the water.

"Why, hello there!" Brisa said sweetly to

the pond's three resident frogs.

The bulgy eyes didn't move. The trio of frogs didn't so much as *ribbit* a reply.

"You're probably feeling too dirty to be polite," Brisa said understandingly. "But don't you worry—I'm about to give you the bath of your life!"

She grabbed a leafy tree branch with her teeth. Then she propped the branch on the side of the pond and pried the little frogs out of the mud.

Next, she gripped a "sponge" made of fragrant, green moss in her teeth and dipped it into the water. Swabbing away, she washed all the mud and gunk off the messy frogs.

But through all of this, the little green guys didn't say a word. Not "How do you do?" Or, "How nice of you to give us a bath!" Or even, "My, what a pretty little horse you are!"

Shaking her head in bewilderment, Brisa paused in her sponging and waved a hoof in front of one of the frog's staring eyes.

"Hel-looooo? Anybody home in there?" she asked the froggie.

Nothing!

"Oh, well," she said to the out-of-it amphibians. "You can thank me later when you see how pretty you look without all that mud on you. You know, your skin is the most lovely shade of green! Even if it *is* a little slimy."

Next, Brisa found a tiny twig. She gripped it in her teeth and daintily began to clean out

the mud from beneath each frog's round, suckery toes.

But she'd barely gotten started when, all of a sudden, the sound of a whinny made her jump. She spun around to see Sirocco, Kona, and Sumatra flying toward her at full speed!

"Hi, there," Brisa said, with a welcome smile.

"Hey!" Sirocco neighed. "What are you *doing*?"

As Brisa got a good look at Sirocco, and the fillies behind him, her smile faded.

"What have all of *you* been doing?" Brisa countered as she beheld her clay-caked friends. "You're even messier than you were after your water fight!"

Sirocco stopped looking aghast for a moment and grinned.

"Check it out," he said, tossing his clay clod onto the ground. "It's clay! We can make stuff with it!"

"Yes," Brisa agreed. "You can make a *mess* with it. It looks like you already did!"

Sirocco glanced at Kona and Sumatra. As soon as they took in each other's clay-coated selves, they dissolved into another round of giggles.

But before Brisa could respond, she heard a feeble *ribbit.*

"The froggies!" she cried in delight. She planted herself in front of the three, very clean frogs and grinned at them. "*Finally* you decide to say hi!"

The frog that had *ribbited* was blinking blearily. Next to him, another of the frogs was perking up, as well.

Ribbit, ribbit? the second frog croaked in bewilderment. Then the third frog began moving. He attempted a hop, but he only stumbled, falling sideways in the mud.

"Oh, no!" Brisa cried. "And I'd just gotten you all clean. Here, let me help you. . . ."

She snapped up her moss sponge with her teeth and started toward the frog. But before she could get near him, a neigh stopped her in her tracks: *"Nooooo!"*

The neigh belonged to Sirocco.

"Brisa," he bellowed. "You can't pull the frogs out of their mud puddle!"

Brisa gaped at Sirocco.

"Why not?" Brisa asked in confusion.

"Sleeeepy," one of the frogs croaked. "Sooooo sleeeepy."

Brisa turned to the foggy frog and chirped, "Believe me, as soon as you get a look at yourself in the mirror, you'll wake right up!"

"You don't get it," Sirocco broke in. "The frogs are *supposed* to be asleep. They've just started *hibernating*!"

"Hibernating?" Brisa asked with a quaver

in her voice. "What's that?"

Sirocco—who had long been friends with the frogs of the forest—explained.

"Frogs spend the cold months asleep," he said. "They bury themselves in the mud, and their breathing and heartbeat slows down. It's how they survive the winter!"

Brisa gasped, then gazed down at the very clean—very annoyed—frogs.

Ribbit! they said irritably in unison.

"I'd be in a really bad mood, too," Sumatra muttered, "if someone woke *me* up *three months early* to give me a bath!"

"Oh," Brisa said sadly. To the frogs, she said, "So I guess you want to go back to sleep, huh?"

Ribbit, ribbit, ribbit! the frogs answered indignantly. They turned and began to hop woozily back toward the pond.

Brisa gazed after them.

She was sad for just a moment. Then something occurred to her that made her gasp! She turned to her friends with a grin.

"I've just realized," she announced, "that the frogs didn't need my help after all!"

"Really?" Sumatra said hopefully. "So you're going to give up on this beauty thing?"

Plop, plop, plop!

One by one, the frogs splatted back into their mud puddle.

"And you don't mind," Kona asked Brisa carefully, "that the frogs are all dirty again?"

"The froggies may bc dirty," Brisa pointed out, "but they're also tucking in for three months of sleep. Three months of *beauty* sleep! When those froggies climb out of the mud, they're going to be prettier than I could have ever made them with my sponge bath! It almost makes me wish *I* could hibernate."

Kona, Sumatra, and Sirocco gaped at their friend, who was smiling affectionately at the three frogs as they burrowed deep into the mud.

"But of course, I *can't* rest," Brisa went on. "Not when there's so much more to do!"

"Yeah, like lunch!" Sirocco declared. "I'm starving!"

"Oh, I can't think about lunch, now!" Brisa said breezily. "I can't get hungry when I've got a mission!"

"A mission?" Kona asked nervously.

"What kind of dress-up are you dreaming

up now?" Sumatra teased. "Are you going to style the silk on all the ears of corn in Leanna's garden? Or color-match every pebble in the dandelion meadow?"

Kona and Sirocco started to laugh—until Brisa nickered approvingly.

"Those are great ideas, Sumatra!" Brisa exclaimed seriously. "But for now, I have something *else* in mind."

She fluttered into the air. And before Sumatra could gasp out, "Just joking!"—Brisa was flying furiously toward the dandelion meadow, leaving her stunned friends behind.

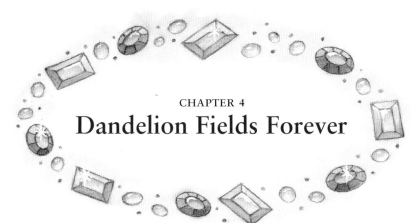

CHAPTER 4
Dandelion Fields Forever

"The beautifier is on the loose again!" Sumatra said in alarm.

"We've got to go after her!" Kona agreed.

"Uh, guys," Sirocco said, following the fillies as they flew toward the meadow, "did you not hear me mention *lunch*? As in, the most important meal of the day?"

"I thought that was breakfast," Sumatra called over her shoulder.

"Sure, at *breakfast time it is*," Sirocco whinnied. "And at lunchtime it's lunch, and at afternoon snack time, it's afternoon snack, and at—"

Sirocco was cut off as the three Wind Dancers emerged from the forest.

"Do you see any animals wearing tutus?" Sumatra asked fearfully.

"Or any plants that are *way* too sparkly for their own good?" Kona countered.

"Or any carrot sandwiches lying around?" Sirocco chimed in, his belly groaning audibly. "If I don't get some food soon, I won't be able to *see* anything! I'll pass out!"

"Listen to the drama horse over there," Sumatra said to Kona with an eye-roll.

But Kona had to reluctantly agree.

"Well, Sirroco's right," she said. "It *is* lunchtime and Brisa's nowhere to be seen. We might as well eat and look for her later."

"Yes!" Sirocco said, heading for the Wind Dancers' tree house. "Let's go!"

.   .   .

"There!" Brisa said. "All finished."

She put down the loop of shiny silk that she'd borrowed from a friendly spider who lived in a nearby tree. Then she fluttered up into the air so she could check out her work.

Brisa had taken a length of spider silk and

 used her teeth to wrap it around the spiky seeds on a fluffy dandelion. Then she'd tied the delicate silk into a pretty bow.

"That pretty puff isn't going *anywhere* now," Brisa said, admiring the dandelion's perfectly round, white poof. "I've tied its seeds tight! Now they'll stay put and pretty forever."

Brisa fluttered a bit higher and gazed out over the dandelion meadow.

"So, that's one dandelion secured . . ." she said to herself, "about *nine hundred* to go."

She heaved a small, weary sigh. But then she shrugged and smiled.

"Well, it's all in the name of beauty," she told herself as she flew over to the next dandelion. She was just about to begin battening down its seeds when she spotted Kona, Sumatra, and Sirocco winging their way toward her.

"Oh!" Brisa cried delightedly. She rose higher in the air and fluttered her sparkly wings at her friends. "Helloooo! Over here!"

As her friends flew over, Brisa saw that Kona was dabbing gracefully at her lips with the ends of her long, violet mane and Sirocco was chewing on what must have been his last bite of lunch.

Brisa jumped as her stomach rumbled. She glanced up at the sun and was startled to see that it had dipped in the sky.

"It must be almost two o' clock!" Brisa realized. "Where did the time fly?"

"The better question," Sumatra asked as the Wind Dancer trio reached Brisa, "is where did *you* fly off to?"

Brisa forgot her empty stomach and grinned at her friends.

"Oh, wait 'til you hear!" she said. "You know Mrs. Spider? Who lives in the apple tree next door to ours? Well, she gave me some of her silk. I'm using it to tie down all these seeds so the dandelions will stay full and fluffy

 forever! There's nothing uglier than a bald dandelion stem, don't you think?"

She smiled at the other Wind Dancers. But they didn't return her grin. "Brisa!" Sumatra cried. "Dandelions aren't *supposed* to keep their seeds."

She flew over to an extra-fluffy dandelion nearby and blew on it. Countless white parachutes flew into the air dangling little, brown seeds. They coasted on the breeze, then began to drift toward the ground.

"See?" Sumatra explained. "Each seed will burrow into the ground to create a *new* dandelion. But if the seeds don't scatter . . ."

". . . no more new dandelions!" Sirocco finished.

"And a lot *less* beauty in our dandelion meadow, when you think about it," Kona said.

"Oh!" Brisa cried as Kona's words sank in. "That's a very good point. And it changes everything!"

"So you're going to stop your beauty project?" Kona said carefully. She tried not to look *too* happy (or hopeful). She didn't want to hurt Brisa's feelings.

"I *will* stop," Brisa said soberly.

Sumatra and Sirocco heaved quiet sighs of relief.

"I'll stop tying down the dandelion seeds," Brisa said, brightening up. "But as for my beauty mission? *That* I'll never stop! I owe it to the world to make all pretty things even *more* pretty!"

Brisa frowned thoughtfully and she murmured, "Now, what should my next project be? Hmmmm . . ."

While Brisa drifted off on an air current, lost in thought, Kona, Sirocco, and Sumatra clustered together anxiously.

"We've got to stop her!" Sirocco cried.

"Shh!" Sumatra scolded him. "Not so

loud." Then she turned to Kona and whispered, "We've got to stop her!"

Kona nodded in agreement.

"But how?" she wondered.

Sirocco spotted Brisa's coil of spider silk on the ground.

"A-*ha*!" he said, pointing at the silk with

his hoof. "We tie her up with her own spider silk! If she can't fly, she can't beautify! Easy as pie!"

"Sirocco," Sumatra said with a scowl. "This is no time for silly ideas or silly rhymes."

But Kona's face had suddenly lit up!

"Easy as pie!" she cried.

Sirocco stuck his tongue out at Sumatra.

"See," he said. "Kona likes my rhyme."

"No, it's not the rhyme I like," Kona said (making Sumatra snort triumphantly). "It's the pie! *That's* how we'll lure Brisa away from the meadow."

"Huh?" Sirocco wondered.

Kona didn't answer. Instead, she flew over to Brisa.

"I have an idea," Kona announced. "Let's make a pie this afternoon. An apple pie! You know how much you love apple pie!"

Brisa glanced distractedly at the violet filly. Her belly growled again, but she tried to ignore it.

"It just doesn't seem fair to sit around eating pie," Brisa replied, "when there are plants and animals who need my beauty help!"

"But," Kona responded, "our pie needs your beauty help, too! You can use one of your jewels to cut pretty shapes into the pastry crust. It would be the prettiest pie ever!"

"It's pie!" Sirocco interjected. "Who *cares* how it looks when it *tastes* delicious?"

At which point Kona and Sumatra *both* gave him a kick in the flank.

"Ow!" he complained. "Why did you kick me. . . ."

Kona looked pointedly at Brisa, who was looking tempted by Kona's pie plan.

"Oh!" Sirocco said. "What I *meant* to say was . . ." He hesitated and glanced at Kona. "Pretty pies *do* taste more delicious than plain ones, and you should come home with us to decorate our pie."

"Well . . ." Brisa hesitated. She *was* very hungry. But she *hated* to abandon her beauty mission for just an afternoon snack.

As she pondered this problem, she gazed at her friends. And then she knew.

"I just figured out how I can have my pie," the filly replied, "and my beauty mission, too!"

CHAPTER 5
Beauty Parlor

A little later, in the kitchen of the Wind Dancers' tree house, Sumatra glared at Kona.

"Tell me again," she muttered through gritted teeth. "*How* did we get into this fix?"

"Shhh," Kona whispered back. She glanced over at Brisa, who was busy washing some apples in the water trough. "We've made Brisa happy!"

"But what about *our* happiness?" Sumatra whined.

Kona squirmed. Sumatra *did* have a point. After all, Brisa had covered Sumatra's

pale-green mane and tail with dramatic stripes of yellow pollen! And Sumatra *did* look fabulous—when she wasn't sneezing, sniffling, and coughing!

And Brisa had woven Kona's mane into so many cute little braids that Kona had lost count of them. *But one thing about these braids*, Kona thought with a grimace. *Every last one of them tugs and pinches and itches like crazy!*

Finally, Brisa had spangled Sirocco's teeth with magic jewels!

"Some of the children in Leanna's school wear sparkly things on their teeth," Brisa had explained as she'd stuck gems on each of Sirocco's choppers. "It's to make their teeth straight, but they're *also* pretty! Don't you love them?"

"'*Love*' isn't exactly the word that comes to mind," Sirocco had growled. But before he could say anything else, Kona had jumped in.

"Okay!" she'd interrupted desperately. "Now that we're all gussied up, let's make that pie!"

 The four Wind Dancers had made many pies together. Blackberry pies. Apple pies.

Acorn crunch pies. And they had a system that worked every time.

Kona always mixed up the dough while Sirocco held a sharp stick in his teeth to cut up the apples.

Brisa then rolled the dough out to a thin, round pancake.

Sumatra measured out the sugar and cinnamon.

And finally, all four horses helped put the ingredients together.

But today, their system was a little squeaky.

The pollen on Sumatra's mane and tail was making her so sneezy that she could barely hold her measuring cup in her teeth. Then she sneezed so hard that she knocked over Kona's cup of flour!

"Sumatra!" Kona cried as dusty white stuff landed everywhere.

"Sorry!" Sumatra said with a sniffle. "I'll sweep it up."

She began swishing her long tail over the flour-dusted floor, but this stirred up so much flour *and* pollen that *all* the horses now sneezed!

"Ah-choo! Ah-choo! Ah-choo!"

"Hee, hee!" Brisa giggled between sneezes. "I guess beauty comes at a price, right, guys?"

Sumatra answered with another sneeze. Kona was too busy twitching and itching to chat. And Sirocco had stopped talking because his mouth, filled with jewel braces, hurt.

So the horses resumed their pie-making in silence.

"What (*ah-c-h-o-o-o-o!*) gives, Sirocco?" Sumatra demanded. "You always cut up the apples."

"These braces are pulling on my teeth so hard," Sirocco complained, his mouth flashing as he spoke. "I can't hold my stick knife."

"Oh, fine," Sumatra scowled with a side-long glance at Brisa, who was so busy decorating the pie dough that she hadn't heard Sirocco's complaint. "I can cut the apples."

But at just the wrong moment. . . .

"*Ahhhh-CHOO!*"

Sumatra's sneeze was so thunderous that she knocked the apples right off the table!

First, they rolled into Kona. Who kicked them out of the way.

Next, an apple bounced up, hitting Sirocco right in the mouth.

"My teeth!" Sirocco whinnied painfully. He reared up on his hind legs, kicking over the cinnnamon as he did. A cloud of the fragrant, brown spice poofed right into Sumatra's face.

"Oh, no!" Sumatra neighed. "Not agai— agai—*Ahhhhh-CHOO!*"

This sneeze hit the pie crust and sent it flying right over Brisa's face!

"Eek!" Brisa cried, stumbling around the kitchen. "Look at us!"

The Wind Dancers were indeed a mess—dusted with flour, cinnamon, and pollen, and stuck with bits of pie dough.

"But it's okay!" Brisa said, recovering quickly. She gave Sumatra a nose nuzzle. "I'll freshen up your pollen stripes in a jiffy! And Sirocco, I'll just fix your jewel braces. And Kona, your braids are still nice and tight.

We just need to get the flour off them. . . ."

Brisa started to trot over to Kona, but Kona's chilly voice stopped her in her tracks.

"That's okay!" Kona snapped. "I'll dust myself off, thanks."

"Yeah, and I think I've had all the pollen I can stand for one day," Sumatra sniffed.

"Maybe," Sirocco said, eyeing the disheveled kitchen, "you could just use all that beauty energy of yours to clean up this kitchen."

And with that, the three grumbling Wind Dancers trotted into the next room, leaving Brisa all alone.

For the first time, Brisa realized that *maybe* her friends weren't enjoying her day of beauty as much as she was.

Just like our frog friends were happier when they were left in the mud, Brisa thought regretfully. *And the tree leaves were better off without my jewels stuck to them. And the dandelion seeds were more useful when they were able to fly free.*

Suddenly, Brisa gasped. Another thought had occurred to her.

If somebody had tied up our *dandelion—the one that Leanna blew on to set us free—we Wind Dancers wouldn't even exist!*

This notion was so surprising that Brisa needed a moment to think. She propped her chin on an apple in the middle of the kitchen floor and frowned.

But only for a moment! Because that apple had given her yet *another* idea! Brisa sprang to her hooves and got busy!

. . .

A while later, Kona, Sumatra, and Sirocco shyly poked their noses through the kitchen door.

"What's that yummy smell?" Sirocco asked.

"And oh, look how nice and clean it is in here," Sumatra added.

Kona trotted to the counter. She saw a steaming pie that was *just* out of the oven.

"You made our pie *and* cleaned the kitchen, all by yourself?" she gasped.

While Brisa nodded and grinned, Sirocco trotted over to the pie and gave it a long sniff.

"Now *that's* a thing of beauty," he sighed.

Sumatra checked out the pie next. She frowned.

"But Brisa," she remarked slyly, "this pie just has a plain, smooth crust. No decorations!"

"Well," Brisa said, "sometimes it's better to just let things be their pretty selves."

Then, before her friends could say another word, Brisa pounced on Kona and used her teeth to unravel every last one of the tight, itchy braids in her mane.

After that, she splashed nice, fresh water on Sumatra's mane and tail until they were pale green and pollen-free again.

Finally, Brisa used her magic to *pop* her jewels off of Sirocco's teeth and *fizz* them back into her own halo.

"Aaaahhh!" Sirocco exclaimed, clacking his braces-free teeth.

"Aaaahhh!" Sumatra sighed, swishing her clean, pollen-less tail.

"Aaaahhhh!" Kona nickered, twitching her no-longer-itching mane.

To Brisa, her friends had never looked prettier.

"From now on, when it comes to tree leaves, muddy frogs, and dandelions," she announced, "I'm going to leave them all be. Beautifying myself is enough for me."

"I'll eat to that!" Sirocco said. He picked up his pointy stick and got ready to cut into Brisa's yummy apple pie.

"Wait!" Brisa neighed. "The pie just needs one finishing touch."

With a sly smile, she used her hoof to tap one perfect, pink jewel out of her magic halo. Then she gripped the gem in her teeth and planted it smack dab in the center of the pie.

"Call it the cherry on top," Brisa said, "but with more sparkle!"

"Brisa!" Sumatra cried. "I thought you said you were going to let pretty things be."

"Well, yes, except where *I'm* concerned,

remember?" Brisa said. She grabbed Sirocco's knife and cut out the jeweled slice of pie. "*This* piece is for me! And with my pretty jewel on it, it's the prettiest of all."

Sumatra's mouth dropped open.

Sirocco laughed uproariously.

And Kona said what everyone was thinking: "Oh, *Brisa*!"

Art Smart

When the Wind Dancers set out the next morning from their apple tree house, Brisa's mane and tail were combed to a gleaming shine and the jewels in her headdress, necklace, and magic halo glimmered brilliantly.

Moments later, the foursome landed on the windowsill of Leanna's classroom.

"Quick," Kona urged Brisa. "Put your surprise into Leanna's desk before any of the children arrive."

Brisa zipped through the window and did as she was told. Just as she breathlessly rejoined her friends, the classroom door opened and the children tromped through it.

The school day was beginning!

Brisa held her breath as she watched Leanna trot over to her desk, her wavy hair bouncing. When Leanna lifted her desktop to put her books and pencil box inside, she gasped!

Inside her desk, she discovered a curly piece of birch bark. And painted on the bark— in berry juice ink and decorated with flower petals—was a picture of a pretty horse with a beautiful coral-pink coat, a flowing blonde mane, sparkling wings, and jewels dancing all around her.

Best of all was the caption underneath the picture: *For Leanna. Here's a picture of me, as pretty as anything in nature can be! Love, Brisa.*

Leanna burst into giggles, then gazed up at the window where the Wind Dancers were perched, her face shining with joy.

And for once, Brisa didn't feel sad that Leanna couldn't see her. She was just glad to have made the little girl happy.

Not to mention her pretty-just-as-they-were friends!

As the four little horses took off for the dandelion meadow, they happily whinnied, twirled, and somersaulted through the air.

"What a perfect morning," Brisa said to her friends with a bright—and pretty—grin. "I wouldn't change a thing!"

Here's a sneak preview of *Wind Dancers* Book 7:

A Horse, Of Course!

CHAPTER 1

Horsework

"What should we do today?" Sumatra asked her fellow Wind Dancers as they took flight over the dandelion meadow one sunny morning.

But before anyone could answer, Sumatra made a suggestion of her own. "How about a dance-off?" she asked.

"Well, we all know who would win *that* contest, don't we?" Kona responded. "You!"

"Okay," Sumatra said, looking around. "How about . . . hey, what's going on down there at Leanna's school?"

The other Wind Dancers turned to look. As they'd been flying, they'd come to their friend's big red-brick school building. But today, there were a lot more grown-ups there than usual at the start of the day.

"Don't they have jobs to go to?" Sumatra wondered.

"Jobs?" Brisa said. "You mean like how it's Kona's job to make our apple muffins every morning and Sirocco's job to sweep the kitchen floor with his tail after breakfast?"

"Not quite," Sumatra said dryly. "People have jobs that take much longer than a floor-sweeping.

Lots of them go to an office all day long."

Then Kona turned to Sumatra with interest in her coal-black eyes. "What do the grown-ups do in these offices?"

"You know, they *work* and stuff," Sumatra said vaguely.

"What *kind* of stuff?" Sirocco asked. As the children and adults began to file into school, he landed on the windowsill of Leanna's classroom.

Sumatra frowned in confusion as she landed next to him, followed by Kona and Brisa.

Before Sumatra could contemplate anymore, Leanna's teacher spoke up.

"Class," she announced, "as you already know, today is Career Day! Several of your parents have come in to tell us about their different lines of work."

The Wind Dancers exchanged excited looks.

Then suddenly, an idea occurred to Sumatra.

"Let's have our own Career Day!" she declared. "We could each decide what we want *our* jobs to be!"

"Sounds like fun!" Sirocco said.

Sumatra's green eyes gleamed.

"It sounds," she declared, "like our day's adventure!"

Continue the magical adventures with Breyer's

Let your imagination fly!

Sumatra

Sirocco

Kona

Brisa

Collect them all!

BREYER®